THERE'S A
TIGER
OUT THERE!

For our gorgeous little band of intrepid explorers,
George, Otis and Parisa, with much love ~ S. M.

For Mum and Dad ~ who always embraced
my creative side ... except when it
appeared on the walls and new sofa! ~ R. W.

Little Hare Books
an imprint of
Hardie Grant Egmont
Ground Floor, Building 1, 658 Church Street
Richmond, Victoria 3121, Australia

www.littleharebooks.com

Text copyright © Sophie Masson 2019
Illustrations copyright © Ruth Waters 2019

First published 2019

A catalogue record for this
book is available from the
National Library of Australia

9781760501440 (hbk)

Designed by Hannah Janzen
Produced by Pica Digital, Singapore
Printed through Asia Pacific Offset
Printed in Shenzhen, Guangdong Province, China

5 4 3 2 1

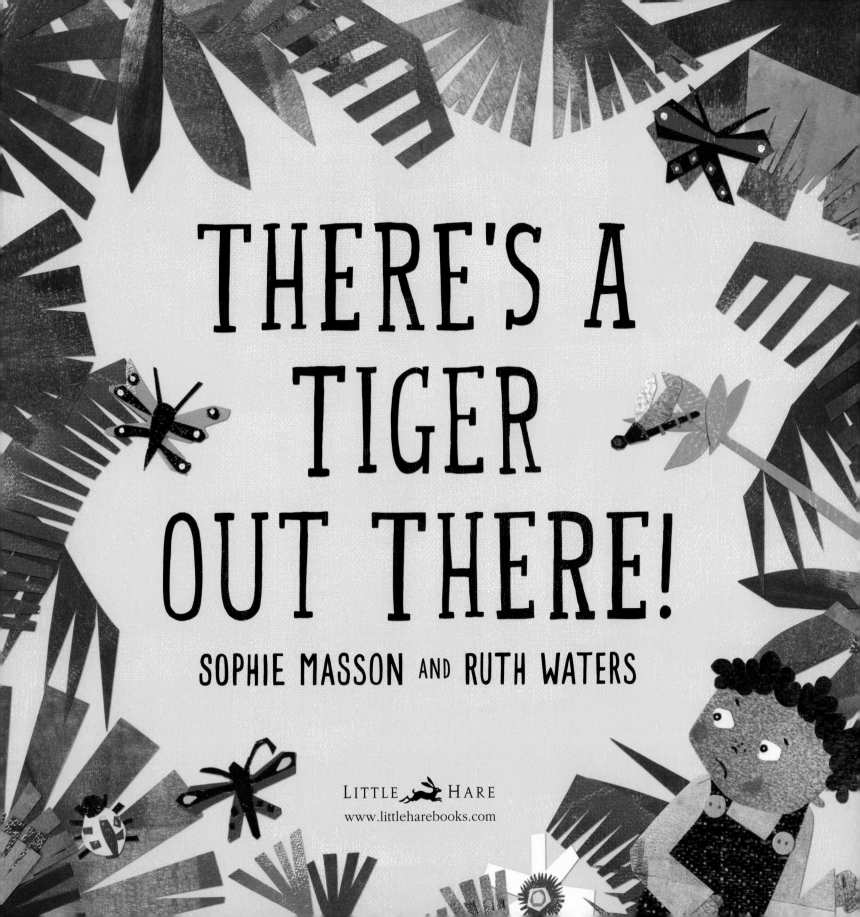

THERE'S A TIGER OUT THERE!

SOPHIE MASSON AND RUTH WATERS

LITTLE HARE

www.littleharebooks.com

Did you know there's a tiger out there?

There's a tiger out there,
sleek as a *shadow*.

There's a tiger out there,
stripes of *midnight* on her fur.

There's a tiger watching us
with eyes as *bright* as sunset.

Come with me,
let's go see.

Don't be scared,
just take my hand.

Promise you won't let go?
Never ever. Cross my heart.

Through the
long grass, just
like explorers.

Down the path,
as quiet as mice.

She's waiting up
near the pond.

Don't be scared,
just hold my hand.

Promise you won't let go?
Never ever. Cross my heart.

There's a tiger out there.
I can see her!

There's a tiger out there.
Yes, it's true!

There's a tiger out there
and her paws are so **big**.

There's a tiger out there
and her teeth are so sharp.

There's a tiger out there and she's about to *pounce!*

Run!

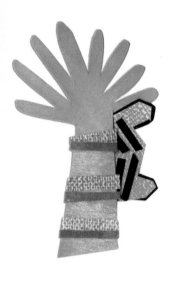

We can see her.

She's still there.

Sleek as a shadow, stripes of midnight on her fur.

Eyes as bright as sunset.

Her paws are big.
Her teeth are sharp.
But ...

... we're together. And nothing scares us.
Never ever! Cross our hearts.